Seeing Faith

When Life Throws You Curves

BEST SELLER

Ebook Bestseller in Women's Inspirational Literature

★ ★ ★ ★ ☆

4.3 out of 5 stars

"A good story about learning how to love yourself regardless of your size."

""A better plan than Weight Watchers."

"Confidence Booster."

"A great short read for women."

"This book is amazing."

Seeing Faith

When Life Throws You Curves

J. MARIA MERRILLS

2M Entertainments, LLC

Acknowledgments

This book is dedicated to Avis P. Gray who taught me how to see myself differently over 20 years ago. This book is for all women who struggle to feel good about themselves in a society that profits from making you feel badly about how God made you. Special thanks to my husband, D. L. Merrills who has always told me that I was a good person and that I was beautiful at every size.

Table of Contents

Act I

Act II

Characters

FAITH SMALLS: A college art teacher in her late thirties, virgin, never married, no kids. She lives at home with her parents.

ESAU: A 40-year-old architect and Faith's fiancé. He works for Faith's father at Smalls and Smalls incorporated, an architecture firm.

REBEKAH SMALLS: Faith's 60-year-old mother who looks more like Faith's sister. She is an older woman who takes great care of herself. She prides herself on her appearance.

ISAAC SMALLS: Faith's 65-year-old father and owner of Smalls and Smalls Incorporated. He loves his daughter and the idea that she is at home with him.

HOSEA BIGGS: A Jamaican architect in his mid-thirties who works at Smalls and Smalls Jamaican division.

ANNA BIGGS: Hosea's 80-year-old Jamaican grandmother. She is known for her prophetic abilities.

JEZREEL BIGGS: Hosea's twin brother.

GOMER: Beautiful, slim Jamaican beauty.

Act 1

Scene 1: Family Love

It is 2012. Faith, her fiancé, Esau and her mother,

Rebekah, are sitting around a dinner table eating.

Rebekah is dressed in formal attire. Today is she and

Isaac's, 40th wedding anniversary, but he has not shown to

take her out. There is an awkward silence as the audience

can hear clanking of dinner plates, and the sound of

glasses placed on the table. Faith is really smacking her

food. The Smalls live in an upper crust mansion.

ESAU: Do you have to smack like that?

FAITH: Like what?

REBEKAH: Like this *(Mocking her loud open mouth chomps).* You act like that is the last pork chop on earth.

FAITH: It sure feels like it. It is the last pork chop on my plate.

REBEKAH: Why didn't you eat a salad or something?

FAITH: I'm starving. I have been drinking Slimquick all week. I can't take it anymore. I have got to eat some real food.

ESAU: See that is your problem. You starve and then when you finally realize it, you could eat the house up. You could have had mostly salad, a piece of meat, and some bread. Three pork chops is definitely off plan.

FAITH: Well it is a special occasion.

REBEKAH: My 40th anniversary is not your special

occasion dear. I should be out dancing with your daddy.

(*She reaches in her clutch and pulls out a lipstick and*

mirror. Then she puts on her lipstick. After she fixes her

hair. ISAAC enters the room. He has a large cake box and

flowers).

ISAAC: Happy anniversary dear. You thought I forgot,

didn't you?

REBEKAH: You did. It's 9:00. When did Benny remind

you?

ISAAC: At 6:00 (*laughing*). But that is not the point, I

remembered and brought you something.

REBEKAH: Awww flowers.

FAITH: Yellow roses? Daddy you know those are my favorite. (*Faith grabs them from her mother to put them in a vase*). I'll put these in a vase for you mother.

ISAAC: I also bought us some anniversary cake. (*Rebekah goes and opens the box*).

REBEKAH: Red Velvet. Faith's favorite.

ISAAC: (*Yelling*) Let me cut you a piece baby. (*He takes a knife cuts the cake, handing a large slice to Faith before he gives the other slice to his wife*). Here you go, baby.

FAITH: Thank you daddy. (*Rebekah has gotten a bit perturbed*).

REBEKAH: A minute on the lips a lifetime on the hips.

(*Faith is really eating the cake in a shoveling motion*).

ESAU: Good lord, I will have to take you for a walk. The seamstress said she will not be able to let out the wedding dress another inch. You'll have to buy a whole new one at

this point.

ISAAC: Take her for a walk? She is not a dog. Sit down

Faith. Enjoy yourself. Esau, I need to take you for a walk.

I got something to talk to you about that happened down

at the office. I want to get your take on things.

REBEKAH: Well Isaac, I thought we were going dancing.

ISAAC: You still want to go dancing at this hour? Let's go

tomorrow.

REBEKAH: That's what you always say Isaac. Tomorrow

never comes.

ISAAC: What are you talking about? We always go out (*At*

this point, Rebekah has grabbed some curlers and starts to

roll her hair to go to bed).

REBEKAH: Always? We haven't been out this year?

ISAAC: Yes we have. We went to go see that movie about the black maids back in the day.

REBEKAH: *The Help*? That was over two years ago?

ISAAC: It was?

REBEKAH: Yes, it was.

ISAAC: (*Nervously laughs*) Oh well, we will go out tomorrow. It's a promise. Esau, are you ready?

ESAU: Yes sir.

ISAAC: (*ISAAC forcefully grabs him by the neck/shoulder*). Let's take this walk son.

REBEKAH: (*Faith is still munching on cake as Rebekah approaches her table. Faith gets up and her mother looks at her in disgust*) How much weight have you gained?

FAITH: Don't worry mama, I got the dishes. It is your anniversary.

REBEKAH: (*With force*) I said, how much weight have you

gained?

FAITH: 15 (*Rebekah keeps eyeing her as she knows that*

she is not telling the truth) 20 (*Rebekah keeps looking*) 30

(*Rebekah keeps staring*)

REBEKAH: I'm going get the scale.

FAITH: Ok 40 mama. You don't have to get the scale.

REBEKAH: Step on it.

FAITH: But mama.

REBEKAH: Step on it (*Forcefully*) 65 pounds. Does that say

65 pounds? Look, put that cake away and let's do some

Pilates. I don't want to be the mother of a fat bride. (*Faith*

bursts into tears and runs to her bedroom) Faith honey,

I'm.....

Scene 2: The Workout

Faith has the stretch bands and is working out. She soon stops, plops on the couch and then opens a bag of Cheetos and begins eating while she drinks a diet soda on the couch. The sounds of the music can be heard in the background. She is also writing in her journal. The words that she writes can be heard by the audience.

FAITH: *Dear God,*

I don't know what is happening to me. Every day, I try to eat what I am supposed to and then something happens, and I get off track. Please tell me what food plan I should stick to. I felt really bad today when Mom and Esau were criticizing my eating. It is like I can't do anything right for her. I felt like I was back in high school again. All the jock kids would stand around and yell (Mocking the sound of their voices) Biiiiiig Faaaaaaaith, Biiiiiiig Faaaaaith. Dad is the only one around here who understands me. Why couldn't I find someone more like him? I guess at my age, you can't be choosy. You know how many single black women there are out there. Mom tells me that she is not going to let me be one of them....

Isaac and Esau enter the room, disturbing Faith's

journaling.

ESAU: Cheetos and a diet soda! That is just great, just

beautiful. (*He hears the sound of Mary Mary and begins to*

walk in place) Why aren't you doing the tape?

ISAAC: (*Cuts off the tape*) I guess she doesn't want to.

Look, you said you would think about my offer.

FAITH: What offer?

ISAAC: Don't worry about it Chub Cakes (*He squeezes*

Faith's cheeks).

ESAU: (*Excited*) Your dad has asked me to help him

oversee the building of the new resort. (*Rebekah enters*

the room in robe. She tightens her belt).

REBEKAH: Did you say, the new resort?

ESAU: Yes ma'am (*Isaac would like for Esau to be quiet.*

But he has not taken the hint).

REBEKAH: Isn't that new resort in Jamaica?

ISAAC: Yes *(reluctantly)*.

REBEKAH: But isn't it being built right in the middle of

Faith's wedding?

ESAU: Yes. Look, we can just put back the wedding. We

have not sent out invitations anyway.

FAITH: *(Delighted but not trying to show it)* Push it back?

ISAAC: Chub Cakes, yes we could push it back a few

months. What's a few months?

ESAU: Yes, and you could come with me (*Isaac is shocked.*

He had not thought about that possibility).

ISAAC: Come with you?

REBEKAH: Yes, I think it is a great idea.

FAITH: But what will I do about my students, my classes?

REBEKAH: You get three months off during the summer.

You don't have any children, so no responsibilities. Draw

Jamaican landscapes, sketch the people; make clay

figurines. You know what you do. Go, relax have fun. We

all will.

FAITH: (*Getting pumped about the idea*) Y'all are coming,

too?

REBEKAH: No, I am staying right here with your daddy.

(*She places her arms around Isaac's waist*).

ESAU: This could be really great!

ISAAC: Great, you say?

ESAU: Well will you?

FAITH: Will I what?

ESAU: Go?

REBEKAH: (*Answering before anyone else can*) Yes, she will.

ISAAC: Well I don't know....

REBEKAH: Yes, Isaac Smalls, she will. Our 37-year-old daughter who is about to be married is not going to let her single, black, successful, tall-dark and handsome fiancé go away to a foreign country without her, that is if she really has any hopes of getting married, right? (*She is almost strong arming Isaac.*)

ISAAC: (*Surrendering*) Right. Faith, I'll put you at Sunset Bay, and Esau can stay at The Sunspree.

ESAU: Why that's at least a 10 minute walk between the two.

ISAAC: Why a young healthy man like you can take lots of walks, can't you?

ESAU: Yes sir.

REBEKAH: Well, I guess that only gives us a few days to pack Faith. You'll finish up your grades and straighten your classroom. I'll get in touch with some personal trainers down there. We will have that weight off in no time before the wedding. You'll be a beautiful bride just like I was. You'll probably be able to fit into my wedding dress. This is coming along very nicely.

ISAAC: *(Mumbling and eyeing ESAU)* I was trying to help her lose that 190 pound weight over there.

ESAU, FAITH, and **REBEKAH:** *(Speaking in unison)* What did you say?

ISAAC: Nothing. I didn't say anything.

REBEKAH: *(Really excited about the possibility of getting her life back)*: Now, I want you all to make an appointment with Rev. Jacob Cross before you leave. That

way, you can have some marriage counseling before you

leave and then you can have some more counseling right

before the wedding. Now, ain't God good? I'll get you

started dear. (Rebekah exits to Faith's room).

ISAAC: Well it looks like we all better get to it *(He looks at*

ESAU sternly).

ESAU: Right. Yes, sir. *(He leaves the house. Isaac exits to*

his bedroom.

Faith is on the couch journaling. The words in her journal

can be heard by the audience. She has schools books,

projects, and papers all around her. She has been grading

when she starts to journal.)

FAITH: That's about a <C>, and I know I am being

generous. I don't see a title. Where are the captions? He

doesn't even give the bio of Henry Tanner here. How do you hope to be a black artist and not know Henry Tanner? He was the first internationally acclaimed African American artist, after all? (She sets the project aside and makes a loud blowing noise. She begins to write...)

DEAR GOD,

I don't really know what to make of the session with Rev. Cross yesterday. I couldn't believe that Esau brought up my eating to him. I know our bodies are our temples, but I am really not trying to abuse it. It just makes me feel good. When I am having a tough day, it's just me and the muffins, or the Cheetos, or the candy bar. Rev. Cross said that I was using food like a drug or alcohol. He said God wants us to get high on HIM. Still Esau doesn't have to be so mean about it. Just the other day, I was eating carrot cake, and he told me that I needed to have the carrot without the cake. He actually said that out loud for everybody to hear it. My mom just loved that. She is around here showing me how to fix flax muffins and stuff. I don't want that.

Rev. Cross did bring up a good point about having children and that I could get even bigger after that. He said his wife Rachel had a dream about me the other day. A dream about me on the beach with my wedding dress and some twin boys or something like that. I'd never want to get married on an island. I've seen one of those you know. While you are having your magical moment, others are still on the beach, laughing, playing music, doing all kinds of stuff. And then you are walking around getting sand all over your dress. No thanks. I only have a good five years left to have children. Maybe I don't even want kids. And twins, oh boy. I don't even know whether I really want to marry Esau to be perfectly honest.

REBEKAH: *(Entering the room)* Is that as far as you have gotten with the packing? My goodness. I guess I'll ask Conswalia to come and help you. Is that a Snicker wrapper? Faith you promised me. I told you if you wanted something sweet that I had some flax seed muffins in the pantry. We can add dark chocolate to it, and it could give you that chocolate taste and some antioxidants anyway. Put that away, please. *(Changing the subject in a cheerful way)* Look what I have. *(She breaks out some exercise stretch bands)*. You can take these in the luggage it won't weigh a thing. This is what you do with them. *(She cuts on the DVD that goes with the exercise bands)*. See, it's as good as weights. *(She hands one to Faith)*. Don't you feel that pull in your arm? I love it, I just love it. No chicken wings arms for me darling. *(Counting)* 5, 6, 7, 8. Oh, just feel that burn. It is really working.

(The doorbell rings. Esau enters)

ESAU: Hey Mrs. Smalls.

REBEKAH: Esau, you can call me mother. I've told you that before. I know I don't look like I could have children your age, but it's my reality. Just the other day, I was at a gas station and a young man about your age approached me and asked me for my phone number. I told him I have grown children. You should have seen how big his eyes got *(laughing)*. I get that all the time, you know.

ESAU: I know Mrs. I mean mom. Faith looks exactly like you, times two.

(They giggle together.)

FAITH: *(Hurt)* What's up Esau? *(He pulls out a drawing)*.

ESAU: I needed to run this idea by you.

FAITH: Why didn't you run it by Benny?

ESAU: She was out. Plus, you usually see things the way that your father does. If you like it; he'll love it.

FAITH: Let me take a look.

ESAU: I'm really not sure of the impact of putting the windows on the East side.

FAITH: Well the sun rises in the East. So if you put it on the west, you might cook the guests.

ESAU: I thought about that.

FAITH: Isn't this spot on top of a mountain?

ESAU: Yeah

FAITH: Have you thought about the north side? It is usually the coldest spot in the building. So if (*pulls the drawing*) you put windows on all floors on the north side it would warm up that spot. Plus if you put some windows here, it would face the beach. The guests could get a nice breeze, and Smalls and Smalls won't create a building that would run up cooling bills for the resort owners.

ESAU: That's brilliant. You're brilliant. I don't know why you never wanted to just come work at the firm.

FAITH: I am much more interested in the aesthetics and the art work as opposed to the structure. You know that.

ESAU: Yeah, well I have got most of my things packed, and I am ready to go. You don't even look like you've started yet.

FAITH: I am grading these last projects. You wanna take a look at them?

ESAU: Nay, I am going to finish up this drawing so that by the time we land in Jamaica, I can take a couple of days off.

FAITH: Oh yeah, maybe we can go to the Dunn's River Falls.

ESAU: Nay, I am just going to chill on the beach and catch some rest. You can go.

FAITH: By myself?

ESAU: Yeah, why not?

FAITH: Well if I am going to be doing things by myself I just as soon stay home.

REBEKAH: (*She comes in dressed in a very attractive red dress*) Oh, baby it is just one day or two, you'll have three more months to do things together. And your father and I will, too. (*She kisses Faith on the cheek.*)

ESAU: Right, exactly mom. Just one more day to go and we are off to the island. (*Seeing Rebekah*) Mom, you look great.

REBEKAH: Isaac promised to take me dancing tonight.

FAITH: So you went out and got a whole new dress? I like the one you had on last time.

REBEKAH: Well, your father has seen me in that one. I really want to make an impact. If everybody else can notice me, he sure should.

ESAU: (*Smirking*) He will! You know what they say, "If you want to know what your wife will look like when she gets older, look at her mother." *(Pulling on Faith)* And Baby you gonna have it going on!! (*Rebekah and Esau snicker.*)

Isaac comes in from around the corner. He is dressed and snapping his fingers as if he has been listening to a song he really likes. He goes up to Faith and spins her around singing Temptations, "My Girl."

ISAAC: They just don't make good music like that anymore.

REBEKAH: (Arms folded) No, they don't. How do you like my dress?

(Isaac is still singing and spinning Faith around. He really doesn't look at her while he answers.) Yeah baby, that's nice. *(The audience is really not sure if he is talking about Faith's moves or the way Rebekah is dressed.)*

REBEKAH: *(Rebekah goes to grabs the keys and jingles them)* Isaac, let's go. *(Isaac motions for the door).*

ISAAC: Here I come. Where are we going?

REBEKAH: *(With attitude)* You mean you don't know where we are going and you are trying to take me out?

ESAU: Can I recommend the cabaret on 25th street?

ISAAC: Faith, why don't you come with us? *(Esau clears his throat)* Wanna be son-in-law, you can come too.

REBEKAH: Well I thought it would be just us tonight.

ISAAC: It'll be fun. Besides, it's our last night out with Faith before she leaves for Jamaica. This time tomorrow, she'll be on a sandy beach, looking at the crystal blue

waters of Montego Bay.

ESAU: Mr. Smalls, I can show you these drawings on the

way. I've got an idea for the new building. Faith can drive.

FAITH: Okay. *(She agrees though she does not want to.)*

(They Exit)

SCENE 3: Relaxing in Jamaica

(Faith is lying on the beach in full shorts, shirt, hat,

and cover up. Esau soon arrives with a full business suit

on.)

ESAU: I know, I know. I am supposed to be chillin'

today. I tried to call you. Why didn't you pick up your

phone?

FAITH: I didn't hear it ring. *(She pulls it out of her beach*

bag.) Sorry, I still have it on silence from the airport. You can't take 30 minutes to relax? I thought we could have spent a little time together this morning.

ESAU: We could have spent a lot of time together if you would have just brought your stuff to my room instead of staying on the other side of the island.

FAITH: We are not honeymooning yet, Esau. Besides, my dad has got people everywhere. I am keeping this trip on the up and up.

ESAU: *(Mumbling)* Daddy's girl. Why do you always let him control you? Can't you do what Faith wants to do?

FAITH: This is what Faith wants to do (*A slim attractive woman "The Girl from Ipanema" walks buy in a swimsuit whom the audience can't see. ESAU cannot stop staring at her*). Take a picture, it will last longer.

ESAU: What?

FAITH: I saw you eyeing her. She is in great shape.

ESAU: That can be you too baby. Look I gotta run. Keep sketching and writing in your journal. *(He cuts the ringer on her phone.)* I am going to call you around 12:00. Oh, you got your training appointment. Your mom called me and wanted me to remind you.

FAITH: (reluctantly) Yes, what is the number? I need to call and cancel.

ESAU: Cancel? You betta keep that appointment. It's for us remember?

FAITH: Yeah, that's right, for us. *(She says in disbelief.)*

ESAU: Hey when I drew up the ideas we talked about, I had problems figuring out the lobby situation. I want it to be different, you know. Stand out. It has got to be different than all of these other resorts. While you are out here enjoying nature, see what you can come up with.

FAITH: I want... to relax.. …...Well, alright.

ESAU: Love you Babe. *(Esau leaves and kisses her on the forehead before he goes.)*

FAITH: *(FAITH takes a deep breath, looks around, and really observes everything. She starts to smile to herself and begins to write in her journal).*

Dear God,

How could anybody ever doubt that you exist? When I look at the mountains and the clear blue water, feel this perfect breeze, I am just reminded that this did not come from anyone but You. It was intelligent design. It was you God and not any big boom that we are taught about in school. I could just stay here forever. I never want to go back to Virginia. It really feels good to get away from the students, from the expectations, well not from all expectations. I have got to think about this lobby deal for Esau, but Why can't I just sit here and be Faith. I guess Esau isn't so bad. I

<u>mean he tells me that he loves me, and I guess that I believe him.</u>

<u>I didn't like the way he looked at that girl though. I want him to</u>

<u>look at me that way, but he doesn't. Things will probably get</u>

<u>better when we are married. I mean, I just don't think that I am</u>

<u>that bad. No one is having to have a crane to pull me off the</u>

<u>couch.</u> *(She opens up a Snicker Bar and starts to eat and*

giggles.) <u>Well at least not yet.</u> *(She starts to feel a splash of*

water and points her hand up to the sky to detect for rain. A

man is standing beside her drying off and water is flying

everywhere. Faith squeals.)

HOSEA: *(Jamaican Accent)* Sorry, woman. I did not

know that I was getting water all over you.

FAITH: Don't worry about it. It's okay.

HOSEA: No really. I've got your papers and your

drawings practically soaked.

FAITH: It's just a scratch pad. It is really no big deal.

HOSEA: Is that Henry Tanner's, "Banjo Lesson"?

FAITH: Yes

HOSEA: Mind if I look at it?

FAITH: Go Ahead.

HOSEA: Tanner is one of my favorite artists, you know I did my master's thesis on him.

FAITH: Master thesis?

HOSEA: Yeah, art history major at Howard.

FAITH: I did art history, too. I did mine on Tanner also. Don't you just love the way he uses lighting and all the spiritual scenes he painted. I just love his painting of "Daniel and the Lion's Den", and the "Resurrection of Lazarus." "Banjo Lesson" is my favorite. It always will be.

HOSEA: Yes, you know scholars says lighting techniques represent the dichotomy of living in race torn America and the color-free conscious society of France.

FAITH: Yes, it interesting. Not a lot of people know about him. When they think of great works of art like the famous Norman Rockwell, they would never think that a Philadelphia born Black man, the son of a slave woman from the 1800s was his inspiration.

HOSEA: You do know that his artwork is the first to be featured by any African American in the White House. His work "Sand Dunes at Sunset, Atlantic City" can be found in the Green Room of the White House. So now you have the first Black president and the first black artist. It's just incredible -- Hosea *(He extends his hands)*.

FAITH: Faith.

HOSEA: Yes, Faith. My grandmother, Anna, tells me that faith is the substance of things hoped for, but the evidence of things not seen.

FAITH: And is funny how I just heard a sermon about the book of Hosea. You know, Hosea loved a loose woman despite her cheating on him. He married her just as God told him too despite the fact that she would never be faithful to him. The pastor said Hosea's marriage to his wife mirrors God's love for unfaithful believers.

HOSEA-- *(He laughs)* Spiritually inspired names we have. I see we both grew up in the church.

FAITH: Church, I should have had a bed.

HOSEA: Faith, your last name would not happen to be Smalls, would it?

FAITH: (*Taken aback*) How do you know my name?

HOSEA-- Why this is a divine appointment. I work for your father.

FAITH: You're in the ministry?

HOSEA: (*Laughing*) No, woman. I work as an architect for Smalls and Smalls Incorporated. Your father owns the company that I design for. I work in the Jamaican division and my twin brother Jezreel works in Virginia, with your father.

FAITH: Ok well how do you know me?

HOSEA: The corporate Christmas card. He had a picture of your family on it. It was you and your sister.

FAITH: No, that was my mother.

HOSEA: Your mother, why she looked so young.

FAITH: She hears that a lot.

HOSEA: So, you are here to work on the new resort?

FAITH: No, just tagging along.

HOSEA: (*Straightens himself up a little*) Oh, you must be here with your father. I would love to meet him.

FAITH: No, he's still back home in Virginia.

HOSEA: I did not know that your mother was an architect. It was wrong for me to assume...

FAITH: No, she is not. The other Smalls is my uncle John, but he is deceased.

HOSEA: Then who are you here tagging along with woman?

FAITH: Esau, my fiancé.

HOSEA: Fiancé, then you are spoken for? All the good ones are taken. Luck is not a good word to describe what he has. Blessing is more like it. A man who finds a wife finds a good thing, you know?

FAITH: Here comes the girl from Ipanema (*Faith watches her as she walks by*). She must live in the gym.

HOSEA: She could use a plate of Jerk Chicken, peas, and rice if you ask me, too skinny. My grandma always told me that only a dog likes a bone.

(*Esau arrives upon the scene huffing and puffing with his full suit on. He has his jacket in his arm and is sweating.*)

ESAU: Faith, did I drop my cell phone here? (*She looks around and can't find it*). Hey stand up. (*She does so reluctantly. Hosea gets a good eye full and likes what he sees. Hosea gets his act together before Esau can see him*).

FAITH: I got it (*Faith had been sitting on it*).

ESAU: You had been sitting on it, and didn't even realize it. You got some junk in your trunk (*Faith is embarrassed and tries to cover herself.*) (*Esau adjusts her clothing. He tries to whisper, but he can be heard*) You got some meat hanging out over here. (*He notices Hosea*). Jezreel, what you doing here man?

HOSEA: No, I'm Hosea, Jezreel's twin brother. (*They shake hands like American Black men do who have not seen each other for a while.*) You must be Esau?

ESAU: Well dag gum, I didn't know Jezreel had a twin. I should have thought something when I saw Biggs on my schedule book. Jet lag, man it didn't register.

I thought I would catch you in the office today. In fact, we have an appointment tomorrow.

HOSEA: I am working out of the office today. Mental health day, you know. I just so happened to meet your beautiful fiancé.

ESAU: Who? Faith? (surprised.)

HOSEA: God has richly blessed you.

ESAU: I suppose ... (*Hosea is shocked and realizes that the relationship is not at the level that it should be.*)

HOSEA: Look, why don't you two come over to my house tonight for dinner. It will be iree. I want you to enjoy some authentic Jamaican food not this stuff they serve the tourists. My grandma Anna is the best cook in town. I promise.

ESAU: As much as I would love to, I can't. I have not made the headway I want to on these drafts. I got to make sure that we can keep our jobs Hosea (he laughs).

HOSEA: Well, maybe another time.

ESAU: I can't go, but that doesn't mean that Faith can't.

FAITH: Esau, I.....

HOSEA: No problem, Esau. I will take great care of her. I am her home away from home.

ESAU: Faith, we good? (He kisses her on the forehead.)

FAITH: (*Reluctant*) Well I guess...

HOSEA: Everything's Ireee *(As Esau walks away, he is eyeing every woman that walks past. He has his lips positioned in a whistling motion, admiring the view.)*

Scene 4: Hosea's House

Hosea's grandmother, Anna, opens the door. Faith enters. She has fixed herself up a lot more than what we have seen in other scenes. She looks very attractive. Hosea ushers her into the house.

ANNA: Well just look at this beautiful thing you have brought in here. Healthy, very healthy. *(Faith greets her.)*

FAITH: Good evening Mrs. Biggs.

ANNA: Just look at those big arms, wide hips, and strong legs. You have children?

FAITH: No Ma'am.

ANNA: Baby making hips, that's what they are. Baby making hips.

HOSEA: (*Trying to get his grandmother off the subject*) Dinner ready gramma?

ANNA: Don't rush me boy. If you want the peas to come out right, they got to cook nice and slow. (*Touching Faith's hair*) You got da nice hair. Why you wanna put dem chemicals der?

FAITH: My hair is hard to manage so...

ANNA: Anna help you wit dat (*She starts to braid her hair. Upon touching her hair again. She pauses and gets a chill. She has received a Word*) You have two big strong healthy boys around you. They good boys but hard headed sometimes. It'll happen sooner than you think.. Your husband love you like Jesus loved the church. Me no have

no pickaninny no more. Anna wanna lil pickne, you know?

FAITH: (*Giggles*) At my age and with the wedding pushed

back, I don't see any children in my future.

ANNA: (*Almost angered*) You ain't got to see it. GOD see

it and tell me, you know.

FAITH: I'm sorry I didn't mean to ....

ANNA: Why your fiancé' not coming?

FAITH: Work.

ANNA: The spirit say you won't marry him no way. God's

got someone else for you, you know.

HOSEA: Grandma, you can get out of Faith's hair. The

peas are ready.

ANNA : I done seen all I needs darling. (*Anna pushes Faith*

out of the chair. HOSEA brings the food to the table and

they all gather round to eat. Anna prays.) Lord, tank you fo da food and fo me daughter who done come round with her big black beautiful self, just like me mother.

HOSEA: (*It's very awaked as he smiles at Faith*) So, you were helping Esau with a draft?

FAITH: Yes. We were looking at the windows and now it has complicated the position of the lobby. He wants something different, very different.

ANNA : Your mother is a healthy woman too, or is she poor looking and skinny like Anna?

FAITH: Why I don't think that you are poor looking Mrs. Biggs. I guess you are about the same size. Why I would kill to be your size.

ANNA: Now you are talking crazy daughter. One time me got sick, I couldn't eat nothing. I wasted away to nothing but bones. Doctor told me that if I lost 10 more pounds me be a goner. If I be healthy like you no problem. I what you call de runt in the family. You know when a dogs had de pups, she always has one runt. Wat dat be me, da runt. All the women in my family big, fat, and black like you.

HOSEA: American woman don't want to be called fat gran'ma. It is an insult?

ANNA: They don't want to be called fat. Well what's wrong with fat? Me think it look pretty. You like fried plantain? You try mine, you know.

FAITH: Now that's good.

ANNA: Let me see if you cook, you know. You tell me what you taste and smell, you know.

HOSEA: *(trying to stop her)* Gramma...

FAITH: That's okay. I taste cinnamon, vanilla bean, sugar.

ANNA -- Pretty good. One thing you missed, you know.

FAITH: Is it curry?

ANNA: - no

FAITH: Coriander?

ANNA: no

FAITH - Allspice?

ANNA: You close -- Clove. Fresh clove. I grow it right

up on me house.

FAITH: It's delicious.

ANNA: It is a secret family recipe, but I give it to you,

daughter.

HOSEA: I have some ideas about your draft. Would you

like to see them?

FAITH: After I help Mrs. Biggs with the dishes.

ANNA: Oh thank you my dear, but I have them. You go

on and finish your work.

(HOSEA and Faith exit to his drawing room. Faith looks

around and picks up pictures and things.)

FAITH: I don't remember seeing a dog.

HOSEA: No, that was my childhood dog, RIP. He brought me a lot of happiness.

FAITH: You didn't want to get another dog?

HOSEA: No, a man can only have his heart ripped out but so many times.

FAITH: And she?

HOSEA: An old flame. She died in a boating accident a couple of years ago. We were about to be married.

FAITH: I'm sorry.

HOSEA: Don't apologize. Everything must happen according to God's will. *(He is seated at his drafting board with the light on)* Now, look at my idea for this. What do you think?

FAITH: Wow, I really like it. So you added two buttresses on the side? It really gave it a different look, very gothic sort of. It isn't the sort of thing that you would

expect in a resort.

HOSEA: Isn't that what you all wanted?

FAITH: Yes, it is. It is very different. But you know, I

like it. I really like it.

HOSEA: Now look what I did over here.

FAITH: Is that a Gargoyle? I don't know about that.

HOSEA: (*Laughs*) I figure you would not like it. What if I

did this instead?

FAITH: You know, it always amazes me how the same

thing can look different just by framing it another way.

HOSEA: That is the beauty of framing architecture and

framing people.

FAITH: People?

HOSEA: Yes, I couldn't help but notice what your fiancé

did earlier today. I hope that you will excuse the

forwardness of what I am about to say, so I apologize in advance, But I don't think that he appreciates you that way that he should. The way a man should appreciate a woman.

FAITH: Excuse me?

HOSEA: Him looking at the toothpick girls when he's got this beautiful queen sized beauty right here (*He moves in closer to Faith*). Why if you were my woman, I would not dare let you have dinner in another man's home, not without me, looking like you do. In Esau's frame, you look like a Don't, like the black cross outs that you see in Glamour magazine. But it my frame, you look like a do -- A pinup for all the world to see. (*Faith is breathing a little heavy. She is nervous and tries to pull herself together.*)

FAITH- A Do?

HOSEA: Yes my dear faith.

FAITH: In my frame, I'm a don't.

HOSEA: I figured as much (*Faith tries to move away to change the subject*.)

FAITH: You know, the resort of looks like a church now, a cathedral if you will.

HOSEA: I see what you are saying. *(He now places Faith in front of the mirror. He holds up his hands as if it is frame of a camera)* Now, what are you seeing? Are you really seeing Faith? Are you seeing the way that Faith sees herself or Esau sees her? *(He hugs Faith from behind and she wiggles past him kind of like Pepe le Pew and the cat on Bugs Bunny. Her cell phone rings. It's Esau)*.

FAITH: Oh, hey Esau. Yes, we have finished with dinner. Yes, I am on my way back to the resort right now. No, you don't have to come pick me up. I'll just call a cab. I know I am in a foreign country. You're right. Yes, it is fine to honk the horn. I'll be right out.

HOSEA: You should have asked him to come in.

FAITH: It's close to 11:00 pm. Where I come from that's rude to enter someone's home you don't know at that hour.

HOSEA: Have it your way Faith. Shall we go back to the living room.

FAITH: Yes, I think that is a good idea (She grabs her neck in a nervous gesture).

HOSEA: You have tension in your neck, allow me (*She moves back*).

FAITH: No, I got it. It's okay. *(Anna's voice is heard calling Faith)*

ANNA: Faith, oh Faith.

FAITH: Yes ma'am?

ANNA: Can you wear this? (*She is holding up a yellow dress that is way too big)*

FAITH: (*Faith holds it up to herself*) I think it is a little big.

ANNA: I can take it up. Now let me get your measurements. *(She measures he bust, arm length, her waist, her leg seem. She starts to hum, " Brick house by the Commodores).* I can take it up and have it ready for you in a few days. Hosea *(She yells.)*

HOSEA: Yes ma'am.

ANNA: Did you say that Jamaican architecture awards banquet is tomorrow? (*Talking to Faith*) I'll have it ready for you then, you know.

HOSEA: I haven't asked her or her fiancé to come yet.

ANNA: Oh, they coming. At least she is. The Spirit done already told me, you know..

(The horn beeps and Faith hurriedly leaves).

FAITH: Thank you all for the hospitality.

HOSEA: (*Rushing to see her out*) I am afraid that I came off too strong. My apologies.

FAITH: (*Opening the door herself*) That's okay. (*He grabs her arm before she can fully go out the door.*)

HOSEA: So when will I see you again?

FAITH: Ummm, I'll have Esau let you know. (*The door shuts.*)

HOSEA: Grandma, why did you have to tell her what the spirit told you?

ANNA: Baby, when God tells you something it's never for you to keep inside. He wanted her to know it. Maybe she been asking God about it, and he giving her the answers through me.

HOSEA: Well I don't want to scare her off before it even gets going.

ANNA: You haven't been hearing what I been teaching you this whole time? When God's got something for you. It's for you. Nobody can change that. Not even you. And Hosea, you ain't gotta force yourself on her so hard. It'll all work out.

HOSEA: What else did He say?

ANNA: What I said is what I got. Anymore and you gotta ask Him for yourself.

HOSEA: (Happy) Granmma, Faith Biggs?

ANNA: Big Faith. Did you see them big pretty legs and those hips (She is fading..) She'll make dem pretty pickaninnies, you know?

Act II

Scene 1: Blossoms

(Faith is sitting on the bed in her resort suite writing in her journal. She cuts on her IPod. The words from her journal can be heard by the audience.)

FAITH:

Dear God,

Could it be? Is this really true or just a trick of Satan?

Hosea was a little forceful which was a bit of a turn off, but he seems so kind and caring, insightful, and wise. What kind of woman am I to go on a trip with my Fiancé and then go off with another man? Are you really speaking to Grandma Anna? I must admit that I like the way it feels to be admired, appreciated, not made to feel bad about who I am. It's refreshing. It's that how you see me? Do you always see the best in me? Oh if I could learn that. If I could learn how to love me accept me, appreciate me if I was seeing Faith the way that you see me.

I want to go to that Banquet. Yes the canary dress was a little big, but yellow is my color, you know? It's happy. It's how I want to feel. It's like that time that I was really lonely and I felt so bad. Mom had just said something about me. I can't remember what it was, and I wanted a hug. I called on you, and though I could not see you, I felt you. I felt the presence of your spirit, Jesus. If I could see it, I would describe it as yellow like the warm sun surrounded in this Jamaican breeze. I woke up the next morning and I felt so good. I only had three hours of sleep that night, but it felt like 10. Can you hold me again dear God? Will you hold me to sleep?

(Faith goes to sleep. The lighting changes suggest that time has lapsed from night to morning. The birds are heard chirping and the Jamaican ocean waves come in loud. There is a knock at the door. It's Isaac and Rebekah Smalls.)

FAITH: (*Excitedly*) Daddy (*She really hugs and kisses him*). Hey mama.

REBEKAH: Faith...

FAITH: What are yawl doing here?

REBEKAH: Your father could not get in touch with you and started freaking out.

ISAAC: Not freaking out, just worried Chub Cakes. Besides, I had forgotten about this invitation to the Jamaican Architecture Awards. I am a nominee.

FAITH: It's tomorrow, right?

ISAAC: Yeah, how you know about it. Esau?

FAITH: No, Hosea.

ISAAC: How you know Hosea? He's my number one architect in Jamaica.

FAITH: I met him on the beach.

ISAAC: You didn't meet him at the office *(concerned)*? *(He gets ready to make a call. Reading a text.)* I see they got the draft done. No need to call then. Hosea, he's my number one. I can depend on him and how he sees things.

FAITH: He had me over to his house last night to have dinner.

REBEKAH: You and Esau?

FAITH: Well, Esau could not make it.

REBEKAH: You went over to a strange man's house without someone? Have you lost your mind?

FAITH: It's okay mom. It was fine. His grandmother was there. She was really nice.

REBEKAH: Is that who put that braid in your hair? You can't braid a lick.

FAITH: Yes it was.

REBEKAH: You know you need to stop having these Jamaicans in your hair. They work roots and all. She might have taken a piece of your hair and done who knows what with it.

FAITH: She seems like a Christian to me.

REBEKAH: Things aren't always what they look like Faith. It's not all about what you see.

FAITH: (*Faith giggles...*)

REBEKAH: What's so funny?

FAITH: Well she saw what you been wanting to see for years.

REBEKAH: What's that?

FAITH: Me, with twin boys.

REBEKAH: Lord, now you haven't come down here and got yourself pregnant, have you?

FAITH: No Ma'am. You know I am saving myself for marriage.

ISAAC: Good. I am glad to see that Wanna Be Son-in-law isn't here up to no good like I hoped he wouldn't be.

FAITH: Now daddy, you know I wouldn't.

ISAAC: I know Chub Cakes.

FAITH: Well, she saw me married to someone other than Esau. Then she starting calling me daughter.

REBEKAH: Oh dear, these people trying to get to America. Can't you see that? They will say anything. They are trying to get that Green Card.

FAITH: I didn't even think about that.

REBEKAH: Well think about it. Besides, you don't need to carry around twins as big as you are already.

FAITH: Oh, here we go. I am going to jump in the shower right quick.

ISAAC: I am going downstairs for breakfast. You coming? Faith you want us to bring you something back?

FAITH (*From the shower*) That's ok.

REBEKAH: She can afford to miss a meal or two.

ISAAC: Rebekah please. (*As they are exiting Esau enters*)

ESAU: Mom... Dad....

ISAAC: You can call me Mr. Smalls until its official.

ESAU: Yes sir, Mr. Smalls. Well I am glad that you all made it in safely.

ISAAC: When were you going to remind me about the awards?

ESAU: Oh, yes sir.

ISAAC: It's good that Hosea reminded me.

ESAU: You know Hosea?

ISAAC: Of course I know him. You know his twin brother Jezreel works with us in drafting department. Hosea, he's my best architect. He is due for a promotion. The next step for him is partner -- *(Frames with his hands)* Smalls and Biggs. *(Changing the subject and gesturing to the door.)* Y'all coming?

REBEKAH: Yeah. I just need to talk to Esau a bit.

ISAAC: I'll see you downstairs then. *(Isaac exits)*

REBEKAH: We're gone for a couple of days and Faith she talking about kids and prophesy.

ESAU: Ma'am

REBEKAH: She didn't tell you about her dinner with Hosea.

ESAU: No

REBEKAH: You didn't ask her about it?

ESAU: No

REBEKAH: Wake up Esau? I think you got a little competition.

ESAU: Me?

REBEKAH: What's this Hosea guy like?

ESAU: He's a dude. That is what he is like.

REBEKAH: I need to see him. You got a picture.

ESAU: We can look at Facebook. (*He pulls it up on his mobile.*)

REBEKAH: I think he has the hots for her?

ESAU: Faith? Nahhh. It is too much eye candy around here.

REBEKAH: So what are you saying?

ESAU: I'm not saying anything just that there is a lot to look at.

REBEKAH: And you? Are you looking?

ESAU: Oh no ma'am.

REBEKAH: (in disbelief) Ummmmh huh.

ESAU: Here he is.

REBEKAH: *(Rebekah looks at the photo)*

WHAAAAAAT. Oh my. This is a serious matter Esau.

ESAU: Hey I ain't got to force nobody to be with me that doesn't want to be with me. May the best man win. Really it has not been enough time for all this to blossom anyway. You know how Faith is. She's got walls up all over the place. It took me years to break through one of them, and still I only get little pieces of her.

REBEKAH: I don't know about this. I just feel a certain way about this.

ESAU: Well just ask. You are her mother.

REBEKAH: We don't have that kind of relationship. But I know who she does have that relationship with?

ESAU: Who, her father?

REBEKAH: Yeah, the big one -- God.

ESAU: Now how you gonna get that information from Him?

REBEKAH: Oh she journals him all that time and writes him love letters. She always has since she's been a little girl. I got to find it. Now where is it? When she gets her a life. I get mine, too. (*She starts to search through her room*). (*She finds the journal and reads a couple of pages.*

She seems bothered by what she is reading. She closes it quickly when she hears Faith exiting the shower.)

FAITH: *(Faith comes out of the bathroom wearing a towel)* Oh, Esau. *(She goes back in the bathroom and gathers her robe and puts in on)* . Mom I thought you and dad went to go get some breakfast.

REBEKAH: I'm on my way dear. *(She exits)*

ESAU: So how was your dinner with Hosea?

FAITH: I thought you said you did not want to talk about it?

ESAU: No, I want to talk about it.

FAITH: It was a nice dinner. His mother was there and she made these plantains that were sweet.

ESAU: I don't want to hear about the food Faith. Is there already something going on between you and old Hosea?

FAITH: No. His mother was braiding my hair and just started talking about twin boys and carrying on. Then she started calling me daughter. I think that's just the culture here.

ESAU: Ahhhh huh *(in disbelief.)* Well, do you believe her?

FAITH: I don't know that woman from a hole in the wall. She was nice enough, but I don't know whether I would call her a bonafide prophetess and what not.

ESAU: So what you got planned for the rest of the day?

FAITH: Well now that mom and dad are here. I thought I could go to the Dunn's River Falls.

ESAU: Dunn's River Falls you said?

FAITH: Esau, I asked you if you wanted to go to dinner last night, but you refused and now you are just trippin'. Why are you trippin?

ESAU: Ain't no reason. Look I am off to work. I'll see you this evening. Oh yeah, there is an award banquet tomorrow. You got something to wear?

FAITH: I did not know that we were going to anything fancy but I can work something out.

ISAAC: *(Enters before Esau exits.)* It's about time to punch the clock, ain't it?

ESAU: Yes sir, it is.

ISAAC: Oh about the awards ceremony, since I am here, I'll represent the American division of the company? I could use you to hammer out the details of the lobby we've been working on. You can have that for me in the morning. Ok?

ESAU: Well I.... Yes Sir. Don't worry about that dress Faith. *(Esau Exits.)*

ISAAC: Worry about it. You and your mother will be my

date today.

SCENE 2: The Outing

There is a knock at the door. It is a delivery guy.

There is a huge box. Faith opens it. And pulls out a

beautiful canary dress. There are also some shoes and

matching purse enclosed. The phone rings. It's Esau.

ESAU: Hey what you doing?

FAITH: Getting ready for this awards ceremony.

ESAU: You're going?

FAITH: Yes, I am Dad's date.

ESAU: Did you find you something to wear?

FAITH: Yes, I have a canary dress.

ESAU: Where did you get that?

FAITH: At Anna's.

ESAU: I have never heard of that department store.

FAITH: She is more of a personal seamstress.

ESAU: Oh, I better get back.

FAITH: Oh Esau. It is nice to hear your voice. You never call to just see about me. This is nice *(pause)* I like it. That makes me feel special.

ESAU: Well you are.

FAITH: Are what?

ESAU: Special.

FAITH: In what way?

ESAU: I don't know. *(Irritated)* You're just special.

FAITH: Alright Esau. I am going to let you get back.

ESAU: Alright babe.

Faith swings around with the dress sitting in front of her.

She is almost schoolgirl giddy. She lays the dress aside

and starts to journal.

<u>DEAR GOD,</u>

<u>I have not been this excited in a long time. I mean it is</u>

<u>like Christmas when I was a little girl. I am looking forward to</u>

<u>seeing Hosea today and spending time with Dad. I think it would</u>

<u>be really nice. I have not gone out to an event this nice in so long.</u>

<u>Maybe mom is right, maybe Hosea just wants a Green Card or</u>

<u>something. Esau is really trying to step his game up by calling and</u>

<u>everything. I think he actually wanted to take me to this awards</u>

banquet tonight. What a surprise? Oh, I am getting confused, but

I am loving it. I...

(A knock is heard at the door. Hosea enters wearing a white Tuxedo jacket and black pants. He is stunning.)

FAITH: What are you doing here so early? Besides, I thought Dad was picking me up anyway.

HOSEA: I thought we'd have some champagne at Rose Hall private bay and watch the sunset and then go to the awards ceremony. You know, your father was running late and asked me to get you.

FAITH: He did?

HOSEA: I see you got the dress and the shoes and the purse. I hope you like them.

FAITH: Yes Anna has excellent taste.

HOSEA: Oh, I bought them and designed the dress for you (*Emphasis is placed on you.*)

FAITH: You?

HOSEA: Yes. Well are you going to put it on?

FAITH: Of course

HOSEA: Go ahead. I won't peak.

FAITH: Give me a minute *(Faith slips into the bathroom and she starts to put on her makeup. She is in the bathroom for a few minutes. There is a knock at the door and Hosea goes to answer it. It is Esau.)*

ESAU: Hosea? *(He checks the door number again)*

HOSEA: You are in the right place, man. *(Esau looks back at the door number and back at him again.)*

ESAU: Where's Faith?

HOSEA: She's getting dressed.

ESAU: Oh, so it's like that?

HOSEA: Like what?

ESAU: You just gonna come up in here and take my fiancé out?

HOSEA: I am not taking her out. I am picking her up because Mr. Smalls told me to.

ESAU: Hum huhhh. *(Esau scratches his head a couple of times. Faith Exits the bathroom looking very glamorous and beautiful).*

HOSEA: Awww, *(He bites his finger)* that dress makes you look...hmmm

ESAU: *(Looks at Hosea in shock and back at Faith trying to one up HOSEA)* It makes you look incredible.

HOSEA: Incredible is an understatement. I think exceptionally stunning is more like it.

ESAU: Yeah *(stumped)* gorgeous.

FAITH: Yawl are giving me a big head. Say it some more.

HOSEA: You act like you are seeing this, this jewel for the first time. Like this is the first time you are seeing Faith.

ESAU: (*Mumbling*) It is. (*No one hears the comment but the audience*)

HOSEA: My lady. The limo awaits. *(He takes her by the arm, and they exit)*

ESAU: (*Esau stands there center stage, looking crazy. He is in disbelief of what just happened in front of his eyes).* Well, ain't that bout nothin'..... (*He is shaking his head). The audience is able to see scenes of Hosea and Faith's Date. Romantic filler music plays in the background. We see Hosea at the awards banquet accepting an award. He comes back from the table, as he sits, he goes to hug Faith and then gently kisses her on the cheeks. Faith is smitten and starry eyed after this happens. They exit the banquet.*

The audience sees Hosea and Faith enter the limo to go to a restaurant at Rose Hall Bay having appetizers and drinking Champagne. Faith is smiling and seems very happy. Next we see them listening to Jamaican music on the beach at a dance hall dancing. Ironically, Esau is at the Dance Hall too, dancing with Gomer. Oddly, the couples do not know that the other couple is there. The limo awaits on the curve.

HOSEA: My love (*He allows her to enter the limo first. He grabs another eyeful as she enters the limo*).

FAITH: Wow best Jamaican Resort Design… How wonderful (*she admires the trophy and then yawns*)..

HOSEA: Wait until they see what we have in mind for the next resort. If I could make it look like you, I absolutely know we would win hands down, no doubt about it.

FAITH: You are a flatterer.

HOSEA: *(She yawns again).* I just call it as I see it. You are sleepy. Please rest. Here put your head on my shoulder.

FAITH: It must have been the Champagne. Wine always makes me sleepy. *(He motions her close to him. As Faith puts her head on his shoulder, she falls asleep. The limo arrives back at Faith's resort. She steps out first and Hosea follows her.)*

FAITH: Well, I have had a wonderful evening. Thank you for escorting me.

HOSEA: Believe me when I tell you that the pleasure was all mine.

FAITH: Well, do you want to come up? I mean I am working on this painting that is kind of Tanneresque. I'd love you to see it.

HOSEA: (*In disbelief*) You want me to see your painting? Right now?

FAITH: (*innocently*) Yes. (*It is clear that they have two different things in mind*).

They enter the resort room.

FAITH: Please make yourself comfortable. Can I get you something to drink?

HOSEA: How about some coffee?

FAITH: Coffee, this late? Well, I guess that I could use some, too.

HOSEA: I certainly don't want you to have any more wine.

FAITH: Huh? (*she giggles*) Oh, yeah.

FAITH: Give me a second. The painting is over there. (

She comes back with the coffee. In the meantime, Hosea

looks around the room and then at the painting. He nods in delight as he sees it.)

HOSEA: *(Talking to himself)* Beauty and Talent *(he shakes his head from side to side.)*

FAITH: *(She hands him the coffee. They both sip).* Cream? Sugar?

HOSEA: No, I take it black and bold.

FAITH: Me too *(She smiles nervously. They sip.)*

HOSEA: You are right, the picture is Tanneresque.

FAITH: I thought so, too.

HOSEA: So, do you have any other work?

FAITH: I did bring my sketchpad *(As she leans over to get it. She bumps into his coffee cup, splashing it all over his shirt and Tuxedo jacket).* Oh my, *(she grabs one of her paint rags to wipe it off).* Did you get burned? *(As she* wipes his Tuxedo, jacket she gets blue paint on his jacket).

Oh, I have only made it worse.

HOSEA: No problem, this was an old jacket anyway (He

quickly starts to take it off his Tuxedo Jacket and shirt,

revealing a white T-shirt underneath.)

FAITH: If I call down to the laundry service and act now,

maybe we can remove these stains. (*She motions to the*

phone. He makes a sound as if he feels a slight pain on the

skin of his chest. She hangs up the phone to go to his aid.)

You did get burned. Let me see. (*She pulls off his white T-*

shirt to see if there are burns, not thinking of what she is

doing. She realizes that the brother is ripped. Their eyes

meet as he understands that she like what she sees. They

start to kiss. She hesitates slightly but can resist no more.)

HOSEA: It's okay. (*He places Faith's hands on his belt*

buckle to unfasten his pants. He picks her up as she

straddles him to the resort bed He looks in her eyes for

consent. She suggests that it is okay.)

As Faith is placed on the bed she reaches for the lamp by

her bedside to cut off the light.

No I want to see you.

He raises her upper body. His hands unzip the back of her

dress, pushing the dress down past her hips. Her dress that

is now on the floor. At this point, Faith is in her bra and

panties. Hosea removes each bra strap gently to the side.

First the right strap and then the left. He then gently and

slowly pushes the bra down to her waist. Faith pulls a

sheet to cover her breasts, crumpling the sheet in a tense

fisted matter. He gently unfolds her fingers and lowers the

sheet.

HOSEA: None of my designs could ever match this. You

are beautiful. *He starts to kiss her neck slowly as he moves his way down from the upper neck to the lower shoulder.*

Hosea's single index finger trace his kissing locations. A

cupped hand forms as he massages one of her breasts.

Faith's facial expression move to tension to extreme

pleasure. He pushes her back gently so that she is now

lying face up.

I want to love you.

He kisses her slowly.

I want to taste you.

He moves his way down past her breast, past her stomach,

past her navel and into the pleasure zone. Faith's face is

pleasured. She has an orgasm.

I need to feel you.

He pulls Faith's upper body again and positions her hips

so that she is straddling him on top.

You feel so good.

Their bodies gyrate. Slowly their rhythm quickens as they

orgasm together. Faith's nails press against Hosea's back.

(The next morning Faith is resting on Hosea's chest. She is

smiling without showing teeth. Hosea has a big wide

smile. She stirs, he stirs and he kisses her forehead.)

HOSEA: Come on, let's go get breakfast. *(He pulls on*

her arm again.) Faith, let's get breakfast... Faith, let's go.

Are you ready? *(He continues to tug on he*r) Faith...

Faith...Faith... *(Faith has been dreaming and awakes to*

Hosea squeezing one her shoulders to wake her. She

realizes that she has been sleeping in the limo the entire

time).

FAITH: Oh, was I asleep?

HOSEA: Yes, you are back at the resort now. *(She steps*

out of the car and he does, too)

FAITH: Well, I have had a wonderful evening. Thank you for escorting me.

HOSEA: Believe me when I tell you that the pleasure was all mine.

FAITH: Well, do you want to come up? I mean I am working on this painting that is kind of like Tanner's technique. You know how he paints with, you know it's like Tangery, I mean, ripped chest and abs, no, strong shoulders. I mean Tanneresque. I'd love for me to see you (*slows down because she is nervous*). I mean, what I want to say is, I'd love you to see it.

HOSEA: (*In disbelief*) You want me to see your painting? Right now?

FAITH: (*with knowing*) Yes. You can see my stuff. I mean my work. That is what I want to say. You can see my painting. You know the one that looks like Tanner's.

(It is clear that they both have the same thing in mind).

HOSEA: (The lights are cutting on as Hosea speaks). I had a wonderful time with you Faith. (*He holds Faith by the waist, looks into her eyes and leans in for a kiss on the cheek. Faith readies herself and moves forward when Esau pops out the cover*s).

Esau has been sleeping on the couch when Faith gets home.   There are drafting papers and rulers everywhere. The lights are down when Faith enters. Esau is sleeping under some covers, though he cannot really be seen by the audience.

ESAU: I am sure she had a good time, too. Thanks man, smooches. *(He nudges him out the door and practically shuts the door in Hosea's face).*

FAITH: You slept here?

ESAU: Yeah, I must have fallen asleep on the couch while working on this lobby. *(He hugs her)* I am glad that you made it home safe. You feel like you losing a few pounds.

(HOSEA is heard from behind the door.)

HOSEA: I'll try not to have her walk so much. I don't want her to lose that beautiful figure. *(Esau rushes to the door angrily.)*

ESAU: Man, go home. *(He opens the door and Hosea is cocked up beside it almost falling through.)*

HOSEA: She left her earring in the Limo. I was just bringing it back to her.

ESAU: Thanks *(He shuts the door quickly, but Hosea is still able to get in some final words.)*

HOSEA: Night Faith

FAITH: Good night *(Excitedly. She loses her excitement when she sees the look on Esau's face.)*

ESAU: You gonna need to go back home till I get this project done. I decided that I want the wedding to run as scheduled. Let's face it. You don't need me to make any of those wedding decisions anyway. You know that you and your mother will do all that.

FAITH: Back home? Well, I was just starting to enjoy myself.

ESAU: That's the problem. You are starting to enjoy yourself a little too much with Hosea Biggs.

FAITH: Well what I am supposed to do. You out here working all the time. The only thing that I got from you was a telephone call. So, you supposed to throw me out a little crumb and I am supposed to be happy about that, like that is enough? Look, I am a grown woman, a feeling woman, who has needs.

ESAU: Look, I was always trying to honor your wishes about that but now that you say it, let's do this ... *(He starts to undress).*

FAITH: No, no, no Esau. I have not changed my promise to God on that. I am talking about my inner needs. Can you see them? Can you move past my size, my appearance, my hair and see who I really am Esau? Can you?

ESAU: Yeah, I can.

FAITH: Well, then you tell me what that is ESAU. Who am I? Who is Faith? What does Faith even mean to you?

ESAU: Look I ain't all that eloquent like old boy, but you know where I am coming from.

FAITH: Well if I knew Esau, I would not have been asking you. Answer one of the questions just one. Here is an easy one for you. What is my favorite color?

ESAU: *(Guessing)* Red?

FAITH: Get out Esau; Get Out. And by the way, I'm not going anywhere. My daddy paid for this room and I will leave when I get good and ready which is never! (*Esau grabs his shoes and stuff when he opens the door Hosea almost falls out again*).

ESAU: Man didn't I tell you to get going?

HOSEA: I was just bringing back her other earring.

SCENE 3: *Honesty Punch*

Faith is sitting on the beach when her mother plops down

beside her. Her mother is carrying a tray of Mai Tais.

FAITH: Oh, thanks. Is one of those for me?

REBEKAH: No, Sorry dear.

FAITH: But you have 1,2,3,4, 5 Mai Tais on that tray.

REBEKAH: Bottoms up dear. *(She guzzles the whole glass down.)*

FAITH: Mama what is wrong with you? Why are you drinking again?

REBEKAH: You hate me. You absolutely hate me.

FAITH: Mama, I don't hate you. Why would you say that?

REBEKAH: Why did you break it off with Esau? You don't want your mother to have a life, do you? I have sacrificed over 30 years of my life for you dear and you go and take a great catch like Esau and just throw him out the window like he's trash. Do you know how many women at your age, heck any age would throw themselves in front of a moving truck to get with a guy like that? So, I guess this means that that you will be home forever. I hope you and your daddy will have a wonderful life together *(She takes*

another drink).

FAITH: Well, I am thinking of staying here in Jamaica,

actually.

REBEKAH: (Excited) You are? It's that Jamaican guy,

Hosiery *(pronouncing it incorrectly)*.

FAITH: You mean Hosea.

REBEKAH: Whatever, you know what I mean. I just

don't know if you can trust him darling. I mean why would

he be interested in you?

FAITH: He actually finds me attractive mother. No, he

thinks I am beyond attractive. He thinks I am hot.

REBEKAH: I think he finds that green card hot *(She*

starts to laugh in almost a drunkard way).

FAITH: No mama, I mean hot. He likes these big thighs -

- you know, the ones that you call thunder thighs. He likes

my big hips, the ones that you tell me make me look like a movie screen. He even likes my broad shoulders. The ones that you tell me to curl in because they make me look like a football player. I am finding in Jamaica that men like meat. This size two ideal is American born and bred. It is what we have constructed in our country as beautiful, and it definitely isn't what's poppin' here or in Africa for that matter.

REBEKAH: Oh well that explains it. I am practically invisible here, and I thought all the men were gay. I am just too skinny (*She really starts to laugh in a drunkard way*). (*Sobering up*) You think I am too skinny for your father? Why, he never even looks at me, and I keep myself up like I told you to do. Well, I guess, I guess I could stop doing so many arm curls. They are so defined they kind of look like man arms, don't they? And look at these thighs.

(She pulls her sarong to the side) You could bounce a coin off of them. And my calves, mama always told me I had bird legs. I just hate my body. I hate it *(Faith quickly pours out all the rest of her drinks out.)*

FAITH: Mama stop; Mama stop crying. Mama you are so much more than your body and what you look like. I mean, I love you. I would love you if you were the size of your pinky or even the size of this beach chair. Mama, those arms those arms use to pick me when I fell down and hold me when I cried. Mama your legs Mama. Mama those are the legs I would sit on your lap and you would read me stories. And those calves, those calves were strong enough to run me into the emergency room when I sliced my finger with the kitchen knife when I was nine. So stop it Mama. Mama please stop crying. Besides God won't even look at our bodies when we go to the other side. He's going to look in here. *(She points to our heart)* The only size he will want to know is the size of our heart. If we are able to keep his greatest commandment and that is to love our neighbors and our enemies. Did we love our neighbors as ourselves? Most importantly, did we love our enemies?

REBEKAH *(Wiping her tears)* Well, it looks like I didn't damage you too much. I did something right with you. You were raised right despite me. Why you got to write so much to God about me, anyway?

FAITH: You read my journal *(upset)*? But those were my intimate thoughts that I shared only with God.

REBEKAH: *(Laughing insensitively)* And me *(She laughs some more)*

Faith is angry and perplexed. Hosea walks up:)

HOSEA: Faith, Mrs. Smalls (*Rebekah is humming and falls back in her beach chair on the outskirts of passing* *out*). Please Mrs. Smalls, let me take you to your room.

Can you find the key? *(Faith passes it to him out of*

Rebekah's beach bag). Come along Mrs. Smalls, you will

get all the rest you need in just a few minutes. *(Whispering*

to Faith) I'll be right back.

Faith motions to find her journal in her beach bag. She

takes it out and wants to start to journal. She picks up the

pen, opens the book, she starts to write:

FAITH:

𝒟ear 𝒢od, *(she closes it quickly and throws it back into her*

beach bag. The audience only hears in her journal voice) I

can't even talk to you right now and I need to talk to you. I

need to talk to you God. Now my mother has even taken

this away from me. *(Hosea returns)* That was quick.

HOSEA: Your mother is a fast walker. I almost had to

start sprinting. *(Detects that something is wrong with her.)*

What is the matter with you? There is something wrong

Faith.

FAITH: Nothing don't worry about it.

HOSEA: When it comes to you. I will worry about it.

FAITH: Did you know that my mother read my journal.

They were my personal thoughts. My conversations with

God. And she read it like it was a public library book on

display to flip through the pages to find out what they like

about me.   I feel so ....violated.

HOSEA: I understand.

FAITH: No, you don't. Do you journal? Do you say all

of your prayers out loud for the whole world to hear?

HOSEA: Sometimes.

FAITH: I mean your deepest, darkest thoughts and

secrets.

HOSEA: Maybe you should not have put them in writing.

FAITH: See, I knew you would not understand.

HOSEA: Perhaps I won't, perhaps I don't. But I do know that the God we serve, we can talk to him in many different ways. Like I talk to God in the buildings that I create. To me each brick is a word to Him. Each building that I design will have a little piece of Him in them. Henry Tanner talked to God in his painting. You, you talk to God in your grading when you try to breathe life and encouragement into the work of your students. To God, it doesn't matter how you start the conversation. It is just that you start it. God is magnificent, you know? We can put him in a confined structure. *(Faith sits angrily pouting. There is long silence as Hosea tries to ease the tension)* Hey it is a beautiful day we are not going to waste it sitting on a beach. We have this whole island to explore.

FAITH: Where are we going?

HOSEA: Negril.

FAITH: What are we going to do there that we can't do here?

HOSEA: Horseback riding.

FAITH: Horseback riding? I've never been on a horse before?

HOSEA: You? Little Miss Rich Man's daughter. Well, today you are going to have a new experience. It will be fun. *(They leave the beach. Hosea extends his hand and Faith grabs it. They exit, hand-in-hand).*

SCENE 4: Memories

Faith is back in her hotel room. She gets out her journal,

opens it, and puts it back on the nightstand drawer. She

pulls it back out and then puts it back again. She pulls it

out and then puts it back again. And then pulls it out and

puts it back on her lap.

FAITH: Lord, help me *(Slowly, she begins writing)*

DEAR GOD,

I feel so much lighter right now. That conversation with mom today was a big blow. I mean she read my journal. She read my intimate thoughts that only I share with you God. But I cannot be separated from YOU. I have tried to pray quietly with folded hands and bent knees, but this is how I like to talk to YOU. Writing is my therapy. Well, you already know this. I did happen to have a fun time in Negril. I have never been on a horse before, and I was scared but you were with me. At one point, I thought the horse was going to drag me across the beach like when Miss Jane Pittman's white horse dragged Ned. That would have been terrifying. I can't say I would get on a horse again though. I just can't trust anything that has its own brain, legs, and teeth. I mean really.

I'm thinking that I really want to break it off with Esau. I mean, I am seeing what life can be like without all of his nitpicking. I really like the space that I am in right now. No, I am loving the space that I am in right now. It's funny, I have not had a Snicker bar in a few days. I have not grabbed this or grabbed that. My clothes are feeling a bit loser too. This is a dream. Weight loss without the effort. I love it, I love it, I love it. I also went swimming today, well snorkeling. At first I was a little embarrassed to show Hosea all of my fat rolls, but he made me feel comfortable when he said, (Mocking his Jamaican accent) "There is not a thing wrong with you woman, but a lot of things right." I never would have heard that from Esau.

There were so many colorful fish down there, orange, blue, bright red and of course my favorite color, yellow. Hosea asked me if I wanted to swim near the sting rays. I asked him if he had lost his mind. Why would I want to swim with anything that has the word sting in it? Hosea said that they were harmless.

I told him to tell it to the Crocodile Hunter. May he rest in peace. I could see me now up on the beach about to die like a beached whale, talking about I thought the stingrays were harmless. God, thank you for my common sense.

I still like the water in Montego Bay better. It is warm and calm and peaceful just like your love is for me. Tomorrow, Hosea and I are planning to go to an art exhibit. God, everyday just gets sweeter and sweeter.

FAITH IS BACK in BED journaling again. The change in pajamas and her hair scarf imply that it is the next day.

Dear God,

How did I still end up with the food police again? And this time the exercise police. Hosea does not want to take me dancing because he thinks it might make me lose more weight. He is practically shoveling food down my throat. He told me the other day that I was losing too much weight and starting to look poor. This cannot be happening to me. Why do all of my relationships have to center around food? I am sick of it. I am sick of all of it. First Esau did not want me to be too fat and now Hosea does not want me to be too slim. I am not even sure that Hosea sees me either. He can't get past the outer appearance of me. I am starting to feel uncomfortable with the idea that he is undressing me with his eyes. You know, he tried to go there with me the other day. I did not know I was that strong. It was like I was on a date with an octopus or something. First I'm ignored, now I don't even get a chance to breathe.

I do really like the food here though. It is always fresh. The fruit is much sweeter than any candy bar, so I would rather eat that, and the chicken is fresh too and grilled. I can't think of the last time I had a piece of fried chicken. In fact, I think I am going to turn into a piece of Jerk chicken, I eat so much of it--Cluck Cluck. (She laughs out loud to herself.) Maybe, just maybe I should be all by myself. Maybe I need to spend this time to get to know Faith. Relationships are definitely overrated. I mean you got to be this thing for this person and then be this thing for the next. What does Faith want to be? Who do you want me to be? I don't even know what my life would look like if I got married and had kids. Who would be there to take care of me? I know, I know - You would God. Esau called me the other day and wants to take me out to dinner. Go figure, right. We always want what we think we can't have.

I don't know why Rev Cross wife's, Rachel dreamed about an island and me in a wedding dress. And at this point, I am thinking Hosea's grandma Anna is way off her rocker, too. I'm finding that Esau and Hosea are polar opposites in many ways, but they are both control freaks. But, If I had to chose one it would definitely be Hosea, hands down. I guess, beggars can't be choosy. Right, God?

.(*Faith cuts out the lights and goes to bed.*)

Scene 5: The Reunion

The next day, Esau and Faith are having dinner on

the beach by candlelight.

ESAU: You look especially pretty tonight Faith.

FAITH: Thank you. You look nice too.

ESAU: What have you lost 10, 15,...

FAITH: 20 Pounds.

ESAU: Why you lost 20 pounds? I really can tell. It looks like you have lost more like 30. You must be building muscle.

FAITH: You look like you have picked up some of my 20.

ESAU: Ohhhh, that hurts.

FAITH: Welcome to my world.

ESAU: Okay, okay, I get it. Ain't no problem. You've made your point about how it feels when people comment about your body all the time.

FAITH: What's your drug of choice?

ESAU: Huh?

FAITH: Your drug of choice.

ESAU: I don't do drugs Faith. You know that about me.

FAITH: I know, I know that. I mean what food is really good to you? What can you not get enough of.

ESAU: Man, this Pepperpot soup they sell on roadsides is off the chain here. I could eat it by the bowls for breakfast, lunch, and dinner. I like to add it to some rice.

FAITH: Just a word of advice from one fat person to another, cause at this point, you have crossed that line (Esau grabs his stomach and is shocked at her comment). You might want to cut back on the carbs. They can really pack on the pounds. *(Esau grabs a spoon and starts to eat his soup much more quickly.)* Esau, slow down. You act like that was the last bowl Pepperpot soup on the planet.

ESAU: Oh yeah, well I'll keep that in mind. Look, that Hosea dude is messing everything up. You should have stayed at home in the first place. That is what you should have done. *(Esau watches some more girls as they walk by.)*

FAITH: Well, you asked me to come. Didn't you ask me to come?

ESAU: Yeah, I did.

FAITH: Well, here I am. All of me, baby.

ESAU: Look, it was a mistake.

FAITH: There was a time I would have believed in mistakes, but I just don't anymore. All things happen for a reason. Me being here is a divine appointment.

ESAU: Well not really, cause Rev Cross' wife's dream didn't even come true. Remember she said we were going to get married on the beach and have twin boys.

FAITH: I have been thinking about that, too. She didn't say we were. What she said is that she saw me in a wedding gown and then saw me with twin boys.

ESAU: Oh, so you think that's you and old boy?

FAITH: Hosea. His name is Hosea.

ESAU: Yes, didn't you tell me that Hosea's grandma said about the same thing and started calling you daughter and all?

FAITH: Yes, she did. I guess she was speaking things that were not as though they were. Wishful thinking, you know.

ESAU: I wouldn't discount the coincidence. But hey, I didn't come here to talk about you being with another man. I came here to talk about you being with me.

FAITH: (*Starts to get a bit rattled*) Esau let's stop pretending. I think we got all caught up in this wedding stuff. I think we both know that we are not compatible with each other. You don't see me Esau. You don't see me. And the only reason why you do now is because you think someone else wants me. You don't want me, but you don't want anyone else to have me. And really Esau, I am not your type. I am not your type at all. You want a 16 oz, and I'm a two liter.

ESAU: (Laughs) Look, you don't have to put yourself down.

FAITH: No, its okay, "Cause what I learned here is that there are plenty of people who are thirsty and a 16 oz just won't do. It's okay. It's a preference. It's a frame. It's how you see the world. It is how you want your world to be. But just know, that your preferences don't represent everyone else's. Some men actually find big women attractive.

ESAU: (*Trying to calm her in a convincing tone*) Look, look, look Faith, when it is all said and done, we, we work so well together.

FAITH: We can still work well together, but just not as husband and wife. I have a vested interest in seeing that the company does well, you know. After all, it will be my company someday. You are good at what you do. Dad knows that.

ESAU: Yeah, your dad.

FAITH: Don't worry. I will smooth things over for him. He may be angry because he thinks I will be upset, but it will only be for a while. Trust me, he knows that you are talented. Believe me, he is not going to let anything affect his bottom line.

ESAU: Well, I do genuinely care about you Faith.

FAITH: And I care about you, too.

ESAU: So this is it? Its five years of dating down the drain.

FAITH: I don't think it's all a waste. I mean because of you, I am finally seeing who I am *(The Girl from Ipanema walks by. Again, Esau gets an eyefull).*

Why don't you go after her?

ESAU: You're okay with that?

FAITH: You find your happiness too Esau. Life is short.

ESAU: (*Running after the girl from Ipanema*) Excuse me, excuse me miss,   what's your name? I'm Esau (*Esau goes off stage).* You are really giving that swimsuit a workout. (*Faith gets up from her table smiling and is about to go offstage when she runs into Hosea. She runs up to hug him.)*

FAITH: Hosea. I'm all yours now. It is over for Esau and me. So now, we can be together. (*Just then a skinny woman approaches Hosea and grabs him by the arm in an intimate way.)*   (*Shocked)* Hosea?

HOSEA: Faith ..(*awkwardness..*)

FAITH: Isn't that your old flame who died in a boating accident?

HOSEA: (*He releases GOMER's arm*) You can go ahead and secure our table. I'll be there in a minute. *(Gomer walks away.)*

FAITH: What, what is this all about? What is this Hosea? What is this?

HOSEA: Wait, Wait Faith. I think you are a wonderful woman, but I am going to have to let your father explain this to you.

FAITH: You want my father to explain what Hosea? You tell me. You tell me *(yelling.)*

HOSEA: Your father arranged this whole thing between us Faith. I don't think he liked the idea of you with Esau.

FAITH: My father? My father?

HOSEA: Look, look, look, look Faith wait, just wait...

FAITH: So all those things you said about me, the compliments, the flattering talk. It was all a lie?

HOSEA: No, Faith you are a wonderful woman. You are beautiful. You are all of those things that I said. You had to learn how to frame yourself. You just needed to know how to see yourself. You are all of those wonderful beautiful things that I said. *(Pause)* Look, look, look, look. I think that your father, he loves you. But he is just one of those type of fathers who wants their daughters all to themselves. He wants to keep you as his little girl forever, Faith. Now personally, I don't think that Esau was such a bad guy. He's a good man. What do you expect? You cannot be married to God. *(He leans in to grab her hand.)*

FAITH: Stop touching me. Just stop touching me. *(With her head down, she begins to walk away. Then GOMER: passes by her. Faith turns, stairs, looks at her and then catches a glimpse of herself in the resort restaurant mirror. She is determined that they will not have the satisfaction of* *seeing her cry or break down in front of them. Before she is*

completely out of ear view, she hears Gomer speaking).

GOMER: Was that your boss's daughter? The one he

asked you to entertain while she was here?

HOSEA: Yes, that's her. Faith.

GOMER: That's a big woman.

HOSEA: Yeah, Biiiiiig Faaaaaaaith *(Saying it almost like*

the school boys from Faith's past.)

Faith has made it to her room and is on her bed sobbing.

Her dad enters with a key.

ISAAC: You know, you should really put that dead bolt on

the door. Faith, Faith, Faith *(He approaches her bed. He*

talks very gently.) Look, I got a call from Hosea. I know

that you know. See, daddy knows what is best for you.

That Esau, he was not it. I did not like the way that he

treated you. I didn't even like the way he talked to you.

My little girl does not have to settle, at least not while I'm alive. I wanted you to see... I wanted you to see how you should be treated. How a man should love my baby. Good daddies know these things. Now haven't I been a good daddy? (*Almost angered*) Haven't I been a good daddy?

FAITH: *(Painfully)* Yes daddy. You have.

ISAAC: Now, I know what I am doing. You got a good life. We have plenty of money; you can go where you want to go, and do what you want to do. Now that's right, isn't it?

FAITH: *(reluctantly)* Yes, Daddy. *(Still through tears)* Daddy.

ISAAC: Huh?

FAITH: I just want to go home.

ISAAC: We'll go home sweetheart. I'll have Benny book our flights for tomorrow morning. You go ahead and get packed, ok?

FAITH: Yes sir, Daddy.

ISAAC: Faith, I know it doesn't seem like it right now, but it's going to be all right. It'll be alright. Your father will always watch over you. *(He exits leaving some drawings on her bed by accident. Faith breaks out into big sobs.*

[The lights of the theatre shut off all at once, creating complete darkness]

FAITH: (*Talking on the phone*) Daddy, my driver is about to be up and you have put the final sketches on the bed. Yeah, I looked at it. I think the lobby will be beautiful. I could leave the drafts downstairs with the receptionist. Oh, you don't want anybody stealing the resort ideas? You'll have Benny get someone from the firm to pick them up?

Okay. (*She hangs up the phone and starts to journal...*)

Dear God,

I was too tired to write to You last night. But I did try to talk to You through my tears. Despite all of this mess and confusion, I felt YOU in the room again. Thank You for coming to be with me and to hold me. YOU let me know that it was all going to be all right.

School starts in a couple of months, I managed to lose a few pounds, and I feel free and lighter in ways more than just my weight. I feel light in my spirit. It is good to know that You are still here for me and You will always be. (*Huffs*) So much for kids and a husband and false prophets. People can make up some stuff, can't they? On a brighter side, I do think I have a new passion -- travel. Too bad that I'm leaving Jamaica, and I never got a chance to go to Dunn's River Falls. Well, maybe next year.

But who am I kidding? I am never going to come back to

Jamaica again, even if it is the most beautiful water that I ever

seen in my life. (*A knock is heard at the door. Faith talks out*

loud and is not journaling). This must be someone from

the office to pick up the sketches.

She opens the door for 'Hosea". He is standing there in a

yellow shirt and a hat.

FAITH: Well, the nerve. (Huffy) I got them right over

here. Are you driving me to the airport, too?

JAZREEL: I can (*She passes the sketch tubes to him. He*

takes them and pulls her to him quickly and kisses her

passionately. She pushes him away, but then she leans in

again for a second kiss. She is almost weakened by it.)

FAITH: Now, you just wait a minute. What about miss

beautiful svelte Jamaican island beauty.

JAZREEL: Who?

FAITH: The one who got in the (*she makes quotation*

marks symbols with her fingers) "boating accident."

JAZREEL: Huh?

FAITH: Come on Hosea. Let's not play games. I saw you.

It was you.

JAZREEL: No, that wasn't me. (*He pulls of his hat to*

reveal a head full of hair. The complete opposite of his

twin brother Hosea) You must be talking about my brother

Hosea and his girlfriend Gomer. I'm Jazreel. I work for

your dad at the Virginia office.

FAITH: (*She pulls her shirt closed trying to close any*

view of her bosom. Puzzled and processing the information.

She straightens the back of her hair and tries to pull herself together). So, you just gonna roll up on me and kiss me like that? I don't even know you like that.

JAZREEL: I don't know what the problem is woman. God, Him (Pointing up to the sky) told me this morning that I gwanna go pick up my wife dis morning. Now, let me grab those bags for you, woman *(He goes to get them. While he is grabbing the bags the voice of Anna can be heard)*

ANNA: (Voice of Anna) Now, what I said is what I got. Anymore you wanna know, You gotta ask Him for yourself.

FAITH: *(Talking to Jazreel)* No, *(She is thinking about the possibilities)* put them down *(She is excited).* I think I am going to stay a little longer. Do you think that you could take me to Dunn's River Falls?

JAZREEL: Why, I'd love to take you to Dunn's River

Falls.

Lights Out

J. Maria Merrills, PhD is a

playwright, poet,

filmmaker and educator.

She lives in North Carolina with her husband and

three school-aged children. She has two

stepchildren and three grandchildren.